Note to Self

MAGDALENA MOON

NOTE TO SELF

A Story

Lunavox Unlimited Publishing

DEDICATION

This story like the others would not be possible without the assistance of Duke Crowder and the kindness of Boris... though that is not the moniker he prefers. Some of the names have been changed for reasons of National Security.

Table of Contents

Author's Note

The following letters were collected from Betsy Kang. I have slightly edited the contents for readers and added a section of my own.

- Magdalena Moon

LETTER 1

LETTER 1

Dear Friend,

There is a cat purring on my lap as I write. Her eyes closed, blissfully she warms my legs. What does she think of her life? What should we think of ours? Is life just the list of events we live through? Is it a list of the choices we make? For this cat, life is the bits between naps. For us, it's something more. Isn't it?

Yes, because you can change yourself, and this changes the events of your life. Every new event changes your "self." Please remember that. I'm old now and what I've learned is that you can do so many different things in your life that it becomes hard to even consider your "life" as a singular thing. The truth is, you have more than one life.

You've become my dearest friend, like a daughter, a mirror, a window. I write this letter to you now to tell you why I have to leave. You've said you want "no regrets" in life, and I worry that the longer I stay here, the more I am guilty of something. You say you're happy, and I believe you, but my guilty stain remains.

Perhaps I should have reached out to you sooner, perhaps in person. Perhaps I should have gotten a sense of your thoughts, your heartaches. All I can say is I'm sorry I didn't. So, I've got to try, once again, to change these events.

After all, when we change our choices we create for ourselves a new life. It's high time that we change it again.

But I also need you to understand why I did what I did. So I'm going to tell you the story ...from my perspective. And I want you to know, at the end, how you can find me if you so choose. I hope you will. The story begins with difficulty…

Texas

My memory of Texas fades, those hot September days, back when this all started - but I'll try to remember, as much for me as for you.

It starts with you cleaning the coffee shop bathroom - the lunchtime clean. You can hear Oliver as he yelps, "Where the hell is the tip jar?!" It brings you back from your rumination about how these soap bubbles work, chemically.

Ollie's being adorable. Thwacking the naked space on the countertop. His gaunt, unblinking stare is hilarious. You don't appreciate it as much as you should - he has the funny exasperation of an old vaudevillian mensch, except the boy looks even younger than his twenty years. Having a crush on a cute boy is totally understandable. Even if his hair is too long.

A few customers sitting around *The Coffee Corner* in the front of the Mithra Bookstore stare at Ollie's commotion. There are some annoyed glances from people at their tables - but little else.

Oliver cradles the little tin-wire sign that reads: "WE BE STUDENTS - TIPS WELCOME" like the dogtags of a lost comrade. He's amazed that somebody stole your tip jar. Oliver tucks his hair behind an ear and he grows more sad, so tired of being broke. He looks at the little tin wire sign with the eyes of a forlorn puppy, he begins muttering: "Jess… Why, why… Jess…who'd?"

Jessica finishes smoothing off some coffee grinds from the big machine's catch, she jams the coffee catch back into the machine, she presses a few buttons, and then strides over to Oliver.

The two just freeze. Jess stands beside Ollie. Jess can only take a deep breath. She breathes, "Goddamnit."

The first thing you'll hear from behind the bathroom door is Oliver moaning, "Come on!" You wipe away soap suds from the sink mirror. This is your job. Nobody ever wants bathroom duty. You, Betsy Kang, are the one who everybody counts on. This is your lot in this life.

You exit the bathroom pushing a mop and bucket. You'll stash them in that little closet cubby on the way to the front counter. You look too young to be a college student. Your bangs are painfully cute. It's really hard to believe you're the oldest employee on duty today.

"What the heck's going on?" you say as you come behind the counter. Tagging-in on the fun.

That's when Jess leans over to you alone and changes the subject: "Corduroy Paul *just* pulled up, that's what's going on…"

You and Jess gaze out the front window of your coffee shop at a shiny new electric SUV - and from it, there emerges this older man wearing an olive-colored corduroy jacket. Funny, the things we remember.

You're unaware, surely, that Jess stares at you and smiles while you just keep gawking at that dark-eyed man - thinking of how he moves with the grace of a dancer. He locks his car with a flick of his keyfob, and smoothly opens the coffee shop's door, coming inside...

Corduroy Paul seems to move in graceful slow motion. He's at least 10 years older than you. And you silently pine for him. Today is the very day when your weeks of occasional flirtation reach an inflection point. And poor Ollie has to watch. And careless, foolish you, you bumble forward, oblivious to sweet Ollie's affections.

At some point in your life you'll look back on Ollie and realize how much he must have loved you. He was your first friend after you moved here from Seoul.

Surely you will realize at some point in your life that when Ollie bought you that bass guitar for Christmas, he had already secretly learned how to play guitar. That, clearly, his plan was to teach you the few simple rock & roll tunes he knew. He obviously dreamed of playing together with you for years. Long after you two would outgrow your banged-up bicycles, there would have always been music - a truly timeless pastime - that would keep you two together.

One must admire Oliver's vision of the future for its clarity. His vision is for you. You fool.

But sometimes we don't see the sweet loves right beside us - those loves that fit into our hearts so perfectly that no mismatches are felt. It fits so right, it feels like nothing. Like more of you. We can forget it's there.

It must have ground Ollie into sand to watch you and Jess ogle Corduroy Paul day-after-day that autumn, first semester Freshman year.

"Hello..." Jess coos to Paul: "Your regular?"

Paul says, "yes please, thank you, ladies."

Then Besty, you blink, and muster: "You're welcome, Paul."

Before you can hop to it, Jess has already grabbed a latte frother cup - leaving you stranded, you alone must talk with Paul - and Ollie is an innocent bystander.

Paul leans against the counter and looks to see what movie is playing silently on the corner TV as he does every time. He nods along to the movie for a moment and says, "*Atlas Shrugged III.* Such a good movie." You look at it oddly…

Jess, behind you, lies and quickly chimes in "that's a Betsy Kang choice!" Such a lie. You've never seen this movie. And you would certainly never pick it…it looks terrible. This lie is Jess helping you flirt.

Paul looks at you, a new type of smile lights up his face. "Hi?" you say. Often words fail you. But today the words do eventually come...and once they do, they will lead you down a path in life you couldn't have imagined. A new life.

"Any plans this weekend?" he asks (mostly to you).

Oliver quickly drops his TipJar gripe, leaps in, and rattles a mile-a-minute: "Actually, my band's playing a birthday party. Betsy's, actually. Today. And my birthday is Sunday. In school our birthdays were always combined. And it's my band. And Betsy is in the band. On bass. So, yeah, we have plans. A concert. Right, Bets?"

"Wow," Paul breathes - in awe of Oliver's lung capacity and uzi-fire chatter. But Paul wasn't really listening, nor were you. You never make a big deal about your birthday.

You finally stop staring at Paul's tiny spot of gray hair at his temple when he looks back to you. "Happy birthday?" Corduroy Paul adds: "big weekend."

You don't know this, but Ollie's jaw drops open when you say: "not really. Just work." You look disgruntled.

Ollie looks like he could scream. Paul smiles: "Once you have a job you love, you'll want to do it all the time."

Finally Oliver huffs at you: "What about me?"

Your brain is absolutely not in your head when you turn back to Paul and repeat Ollie's question: "Yeah, what about you? Do you love what you do?"

Paul nods, *yes*. "Yes. I feel like an explorer. It's exciting. I love it, yeah. I really love it."

Oliver meekly offers from behind: "It's our birthday week, Bets. Betsy?" And then, simply: "We're playing."

"You teach, right?" Ignoring Ollie, you stay locked-in on Paul. This is the longest conversation you've ever had with your older silent crush.

Paul tells you he works at the University's Physics Lab, that it's not a teaching job, "per se" but as he talks, you're simply wondering how can Corduroy Paul be cool, beautiful, *and* smart --

Oliver again tries to get your attention: “Betsy, we don’t play ‘til after your shift. It’s a celebration.”

Even if you don’t, Corduroy Paul hears the angst in Ollie’s voice. Paul asks: “Where’s the show?”

“Here. The little stage under the TV. Betsy will be there on bass...Right?!”

You and Paul keep locking eyes - because now you’re alert again and clearly not done exploring this idea. You ask: “What do you *do* that you love it so much? I mean... I’d kill for that.”

Paul leans toward you -- Behind you, Jess is done with Corduroy Paul’s coffee but she keeps it back - letting you roll with this conversation. Paul asks with a wry smile: “You don’t like *all this*?”

You chuckle. “It pays for college.” You consider it...“There’s things I hate, for sure.”

Oliver literally squeaks in disbelief. This whole conversation is killing him. He yelps, “what!?”

“I’m the only one who ever cleans the bathrooms,” you explain. “It has to get done, and it’s only me that does it-”

Oliver pushes back, “There’s things *I* do that you don’t.” Then Ollie adds, to Paul: “I take out the trash!”

“We all take out the trash,” chimes in Jess, as she hands Paul his coffee. “Oliver’s lying. Betsy’s the absolute best.”

Paul takes the coffee from Jess and thanks her.

Then, to Oliver, Paul says with a note of goodbye: "And happy birthday."

You blurt "Thanks." The reason you never make a big deal out of your own birthday is partly because every year, for weeks before his own, Ollie always makes such a giant fuss about his birthday. It's grown to strike you as unseemly to push people around you into being cheerleaders for you.

On the other hand, Ollie does always make his birthday into a fun group activity for all his friends, so his heart is in the right place and you forgive him. Though this year, his present to everyone, and himself, requires a lot from you. Playing bass is not easy.

Finally to you, Paul tilts his head. "By the way…If you want to know what I do, I'd be happy to show you."

Jess hides her smile. You can't breathe.

Paul continues, pointing at Oliver's tin wire sign, "you're a student? At A&M?"

You don't know how to talk. Jess has to kick your foot. You blurt out: "the Junior College."

Paul begins digging into his wallet. "Still. Take this…" He pulls out a business card. "Shoot me an email. My assistant will set up a time."

You take and look at the card. The logo in the corner is not A&M University. It's some Science Foundation. You learn that Corduroy Paul's last name is Gersh. Paul Gersh. When you finally take your eyes off his phone number and his email address, to look at him again, he's waiting for it. Smiling.

"Life's too short to *not* do what you love, Betsy Kang."

You say, “thank you.”

Before turning, Paul compliments the movie one more time: “Great choice” Paul points at *Atlas Shrugged.*

And with that, Paul leaves. You watch him go outside. Jess plucks the business card from your fingers. Paul’s silent SUV pulls away, and then, finally, you look at Jess.

“Oh my God,” you and Jess both say at the same time.

Before you girls can geek-out, forlorn Oliver tries to get serious again. “Betsy...We’re playing Sunday. You know this, right?”

You assure Ollie you know. That it’s all fine. But you grab back Paul’s business card. You continue, to Jess: “What should I do?”

“Email him,” she says.

“I should write him something proper. Not like ‘where u at? …Like a - what do you call it - a cover letter.”

Jess strongly suggests there’s no need to be formal, that Paul was totally flirting.

In honest disbelief you say, “Nooooo... Really?”

Jess shoots back: “Yes” as Ollie offers “No.”

You choose to believe Jess. That was the beginning of the end - and the end of your beginning. I’m sorry for that.

The Beginning

For the last hour of your shift you feel like you have never felt before. You feel excited, anxious, you feel every inch of your skin, you feel a confidence so powerful it's as if your every movement is in harmony with the spinning of the Earth. This feeling of emotional vertigo is called romance. Your mind races: has all this flirtation been building to something real? Is something actually romantic about to happen to you? Even...sexual? As sure as the spinning Earth, you suspect it might.

You go to head back to campus for a study group before your 1:30 class, but you can't find your keys! Oliver is still bristling with anger and pain at you - even while he helps look for your missing car keys.

You text a classmate to warn them that you're running late, and then you get a text message from an unknown number that says: "The Panda's Thumb" - which sounds like total jibberish and you ignore it. You figure that it's probably from one of the moochers in your study group who never organizes meetings.

Offhandedly, you ask Jess and Oliver "what's the panda's thumb?" Blank stares. Shrugs.

Finally, Oliver offers to drive you to campus, he's surely trying to get time alone with you, but you're still so oblivious to his feelings. The boy earnestly wants to keep from losing you to Corduroy Paul.

But Jess complains loudly that she'd be left alone if Ollie leaves. So you make peace by saying you'll use a ride-share app. Sometimes you are so kind so easily, and in the same moment, so oblivious. Poor Ollie.

You leave the coffee shop without even for a moment wondering who put on the horrible movie "Atlas Shrugged," or maybe you assume that some customer did it as a prank.

Rehnquist

Your Community College campus is small and flat. The trees in the courtyards were planted when it was built, so they're still not tall enough to provide meaningful shade. The only place to hide from the Texas sun is inside. The quad is nothing more than people rushing from building to building in straight zips to flee the heat and glare.

Inside is where you meet your study group, as always, in a seating area on orange industrial couches. You apologize for being late, and that you couldn't find the panda's thumb. There's a few chuckles, somebody quips a sarcastic compliment at your excuse and then you get down to reviewing the "facts sheet" which the group shares to prep for class.

The half-hour with your classmates prepping for class is pointless for you because your mind is on Corduroy Paul. Enrolling in this elective class is only for the diploma requirement - you hate it. It's Government and Politics, and you, Betsy Kang, know nothing about politics yet.

You'll realize later in life that this teacher is an idiot. You hate this class because it feels instinctively to you like nonsense. It is. The teacher is presenting a fairytale of government as if judges have no political opinions. They are people. All people have opinions. Nothing, you will learn, nothing is neutral. Even the neutron carries a negative charge at its inner and outer edges with a positive charge in-between. But your study of science is not on that level yet. You will someday have strong opinions about even that.

You get a text message. You check your phone. It reads: "Rehnquist voter intimidation in AZ." This is something that you will later look up. It makes little sense to you now. You grunt aloud in confusion. The teacher sees you looking at your phone and he calls on you, asking what you're doing.

You say: "I was just wondering about Rehnquist and voter intimidation in Arizona." You're not lying. You honestly do wonder where this message is coming from and what the heck it means.

In the classroom, the pause is excruciating. A few students look back at you with smirking appreciation - unbeknownst to you, you're picking a fight with the teacher.

The teacher is forced to concede that you're right. Other students gleefully pile on that a Supreme Court Justice got his start as a goon scaring non-white people away from the voting booth. Embarrassed by the facts, the teacher loses his temper a little, and he directs you to stop searching the internet for "gotchas...it's rude."

Panda's Thumb

You grab a ride from a classmate, she drops you off back at the coffee shop. On the way, you text a response to the weird Rehnquist message, "???" That sums it up.

Suddenly you get another text message from that mysterious private number. The text message says: "Panda's Thumb book."

You text back "who is this?"

"Stephen Jay Gould" is the reply.

You search social media for Stephen Jay Gould - why is he texting you? Who is he? You discover that actually Gould was an author. He's dead. You tell your classmate you think your phone got hacked.

When you go back to the coffee shop, Ollie tells you that some lady found your keys in the bathroom. You must have dropped them when cleaning.

You look at the coffee shop's bookshelf. There, you find an old library copy of "The Panda's Thumb" by Gould. You've never noticed this book before. It's a collection of science essays. You've never heard of any of this - you take it with you when you go home.

Who wants you to read this?

Before you leave, Ollie asks you if you're free to practice the setlist tonight. The show! There's only a few days before you have to play those songs for a crowd at his birthday. You dread the show. You're not ready and Ollie isn't all that great a musician either. But Sunday is his birthday and what he wants for his birthday... is to be a rockstar. It's almost sweet.

The "show" is merely at The Coffee Corner's monthly open mic night. There will be other performers and poetry readers. Usually the crowd is small, but Ollie is promising a big audience.

You tell yourself that letting him teach you these songs is your birthday present to him. But when Ollie asks to practice tonight, you have to decline. Getting yelled at by a teacher today has kicked your butt into being "*super student*" again, and you're going to make up for today's embarrassment.

So you ask if you can practice with Ollie tomorrow. He's thrilled. He chirps that he'll pick you up at 6 and have pizza in his garage - where you and his roommate Lubu, a drumming web-designer, sometimes pretend to be rock stars.

When you get home to your grandmother, she is excited because she has made you a traditional Korean birthday soup. She is happy to watch you eat the *miyeok-guk* and she gives you traditional Korean blessings while you eat. Some of what she says is an old fashioned kind of Korean and you don't completely understand it all. But you keep muttering thank you, "gamsahabnida," between bites, each bite urged on by *Halmeoni*. She's very sweet.

And then she's very funny when the instant her TV show begins in the living room, she hurries away to sit on the floor in front of the couch to watch.

She is obsessed with her TV habits. One is Korean melodramas and Korean singing competitions. Her other TV habit is the most American thing about her: the Dallas Cowboys. For some reason she pegged the Cowboys as American and decided to love them. If you're home when there's a game on, she makes you sit and watch with her.

Tonight it's the Cowboys. You used to hate it...and you're still not a "fan" of football, her cute zeal has worn down your defenses. You know you should hang out in the living room for a little bit, but if you start the game with her, she'll never let you go and you have GOT to prep for class.

So after you clean up, you go to your room to study. You don't read "The Panda's Thumb," you leave it in your bag. Instead, you study a lifeless book about how

Capitol Hill in Washington D.C. functions. You are right to consider dropping this class. It's so boring. You fall asleep reading the chapter.

Piltdown

The next morning you open the coffee shop. You're behind the counter reading while under the TV, Ollie and a customer stand watching a sports news network, musing in exasperated tones about how the Cowboys apparently got blown away by the worst team last night.

You're reading "The Panda's Thumb" and enjoying it - it's much more fun than the boring school reading last night.

Suddenly you get another text message that says "piltdown."

You're baffled, but you remember that you just saw that word in the "Panda's Thumb" book's Table of Contents - one of the essays is called Piltdown Revisited. You're in the middle of typing into your phone another "WTF WHO DIS?" reply when the door opens and Corduroy Paul enters waving hello.

Corduroy Paul does sometimes come in early, and today you're lucky to be opening alone. He remembers your name, "Betsy Kang" he says. He also remembers that he gave you his card and he asks if you're going to email him. You say, "I - Of course! I just - got really busy with school yesterday…"

"What *is* your major?" he asks while looking at the book you're reading, "what's that?"

"The Panda's Thumb," you say.

Corduroy Paul absolutely beams, he gushes that he loves Stephen Jay Gould. He sighs heavily and asks what your favorite is so far.

"Piltdown-" pops out of your mouth.

"Oh my God, me too! Me too!" He looks so happy. And you can't stop smiling. His hair is wonderful. "Damn, Betsy," he gushes, "isn't it so good?"

You just nod and say "yeah" and "it's so good" in rotation a few times...You have no idea.

He says, "I love how it all started as a joke that got so far out of hand…" then he starts laughing. So you have to laugh too.

Carefully you add, "so funny…"

"Absolutely." He looks at you thinking. "It grows into this massive...*thing*."

You say: "It's so good." And then you add, "Stephen Jay Gould." Still, you have no idea.

"So true," he agrees with the reverent way you spoke the author's name. "Absolutely right."

You are out of ideas. You look at the book. Then you remember, "piltdown." That's what you say.

"That's your favorite essay?"

"Yup. Piltdown...Revisited" you say in time because you've, thank God, found the Table of Contents again.

"I think that's mine too," he says.

"Great minds think alike."

Paul smiles, nodding. You nod along. As if the two of you share some great secret. If only he knew…

“So you’re a science major, Betsy?”

“Undecided,” you say.

He’s surprised. “Boy. I think...if you like Gould, you should -- you know what…” he considers. “I work in the Sciences. I get to work with people who were colleagues with Stephen Jay Gould.”

You swear gently to establish a bit of familiarity with Paul and communicate awe of Gooltz, or Goulds, or whatever.

“Like you said,” you repeat: “Life's too short to do something you don't love. That's what you said.”

“Sounds like me.” And then he continues, “I think you would like working in the sciences. Have you ever seen a working lab? You'd love it.”

He is presumptuous but he is not wrong. Without thinking you blurt, “Okay.” Your mind begins to work again and you vocalize it: “All right, so, then…”

“What time do you get off work, I can swing by.” But your natural defense instincts kick in - excusing yourself that you’re working a double, and how you need to take all the shifts you can - gotta pay for classes. That’s why you’re only a *part-time* student...

Paul says, “Right, well if you become a lab assistant you won't have to worry about any of that stuff.”

Again you tell him that you’re *not at* A&M, that you’re at the nearby Community College. He insists that it doesn’t matter, that what he’s saying is: “Betsy, you should see the lab where I work and tell me if you like it. Tell me if you don’t think you might be happier working *at the Desertron* - than you are here.”

You look around at the tables that need wiping down. You remember what he said: "You feel like an explorer."

"That's right. That's exactly right." It seems like he's hiring…

"Okay." You cave, you say you'll drive there after work. He digs into his wallet and pulls out his employee ID and copies down the address onto a paper menu, stacked by the counter. You tell him you can't stay too late. He concurs, he can't either, "Try to get there by 5."

"Perfect," you say.

"Beautiful."

You blush. "Thanks."

"My pleasure." This goodbye goes on, quite long, neither of you seem to want to end it...

Then he adds he'll have his regular. You forgot that you work in a coffee shop.

You make him a coffee. He asks why no movie - the TV is back onto Sports news TV. You check your phone for a text message - nothing. So you say, "what do you recommend?"

He suggests "Patton." That's when Jess comes in. She asks if she can help him, and he says no, that he's got you.

Jess comes around the counter and catches your eye when she slips out: "You got him?"

You finish up the coffee, smile at Jess.

When you hand him his coffee he says, "I'll see you later this afternoon, Betsy."

Jess is flabbergasted and a little confused as she just stands there, watching you wave goodbye. She looks at you. You sit down onto the stool behind the counter and pretend that you're just going back to your book, like no big deal. Jess stops that ruse right in its tracks. She exhorts you to tell her what the hell happened!

You try to keep it cool, saying it's a work-study thing at the lab. You say you're simply taking him up on the interview offer. Jess doesn't believe you. But then she latches on to the thought that you'd leave the coffee shop. You assure her that there's no way you're qualified. You don't have a Bachelors in Science, let alone a Masters Degree, or a PhD.

But then you pause and say, "Jess, I gotta tell you something, though. Something weird is happening…" You pick up your phone. "I've been getting these really weird text messages. It started yesterday…"

"What?"

"Oh, I don't know," you trail off... You let it go.

Are you scared you'll break the spell? Is that why you keep this secret? Later in the afternoon alone in the bathroom, you finally do take out your phone and text back a message to that mystery number: "?!" That says it all.

"Don't wear red" is the reply. You decide that somebody is helping make you and Paul into a couple. If this is a miracle, you're going to let it happen. It's that simple.

Beautiful Red

You're respectably early when you pull up to the security kiosk on the long driveway and find that your name is on a list. You are wearing a blue dress when you walk into the lobby to find that Corduroy Paul has come to meet you. You shake his hand. You carry a black leather binder, you have a resume inside and some notebook paper. When you prepared all these interview accoutrements earlier at the house, you were convincing yourself that this was a professional meeting, and nothing more...If that was true, then why did you take such care with your lipstick? We know why.

Paul compliments your punctuality. He says you're overdressed, but that you look sharp. He explains that the facility is still under construction so there are still some areas where dust and dirt get on everything, so his colleagues tend to dress down. He explains that "the Desertron" is a Superconducting Super Collider, and that the 54-mile long tunnel is nearly done.

The tunnel, Paul explains, goes in a giant circle all around the county and will eventually shoot particles at ridiculous speeds in opposite directions, increasing the particles' speed with electromagnets, until the particles are redirected to collide with each other. Once they crash into each other, specialized sensors in the crash chamber where the collision occurs will take an inventory of what subatomic fragments explode out of the energy burst…

It makes sense to you but you wonder why? "*Why*" is the most important question.

Paul's answer is a very long redundant love letter to the spirit of exploring the cosmos: "Why climb the mountain? Because it's there." Absurd? Insane? A sensible response? Yes.

Explorers embrace that simple answer as the best answer. *Why not?* It's a choice. It's the same choice that brought humans to Australia, that landed us on the moon, brought international trade. Why not. By the end of Paul's dissertation you are with him in his little office, having been shown a wing of the dig site that is still being reinforced with cement and steel and tons of lumber.

Elsewhere in the office building, he showed you a scale model of the final design. He's shared a cup of tea with you from the kitchenette water cooler. You sip it in his office. His office is cluttered with giant accounting books. Were you expecting microscopes?

Paul's advice for you is to take the application he hands you and fill it out. You don't say you've brought a resume. He suggests you take a job as an administrative assistant to one of the Laboratory Managers while finishing your science degree. Once you have your degree, Paul says they can give you one of the laboratory assistant slots. He adds that it's always easier to get a good job somewhere once you're already inside. On this, Paul is absolutely right. (It's really not possible without connections and your Junior College bought you none.)

Paul says that you can work on unlocking the secrets of the cosmos while going to A&M for your Masters Degree. Once you have your masters you can get one of the slots for a Project Associate. By then, he says matter-of-factly, you'll know what projects at the *Desertron* appeal to you most. Then while working on a project at one of the labs, you can continue going to school for your PhD. Once you have your PhD, you can apply for one of the

Project Manager slots. You could do all this in less than 10 years, he says.

Madness. It's so hard to wrap your head around all he's presenting you. A version of your entire twenties on this track. It's impossible to imagine yourself at 29. The notion that a decade goes by pretty fast sounds like a joke. It's not.

But equally ridiculous is Paul's idea that you can work *full-time* and go to school *nearly* full-time, for years and years and years. There is no time for anything approaching a normal life: no time for vacations, no time for weekends, no time for friendships, no time for love -- even if that love is a co-worker at the lab. But I'm getting ahead of myself…You can already imagine how impossible work/life balance would be. Even if I couldn't.

Finally, Paul asks about you and you give him your speech. You tell him about how your parents had moved here to America and you were born here. They moved your grandmother out eventually too. She loved it here more than they did. She'd never seen anything like arid Texas. When they took you back to Seoul after elementary school, they left your grandmother here because she wanted to stay - she adored the wide-open space, the anonymity. When you were eighteen, you forced your parents to allow you to leave Seoul and your parents' tiny tower apartment. You wanted to come back to these big open vistas, you asked to move in with your *Halmeoni* in her little Texas home.

Here you could be reunited with your elementary school friends, like Oliver. Here you could finish high school and apply to college. Your grandmother spends her days cooking meals and packing her fridge tight with tupperware containers of many different meals. She watches the Dallas Cowboys and Korean TV while sitting on the floor in front of the daybed couch while working on projects: Darning a sock, super-gluing a broken can opener. There are clusters of her projects all over her house. Some actually get done. She is a tinkerer. You are like her in this way, but you don't understand how yet. Sometimes you get home and she is already asleep on the daybed couch.

By the time you've told him your life's story, the sunset is painting the sky in swaths of reds and oranges. You both remark on how beautiful it is. He takes you to the roof deck where one hundred miles of Texas slopes off to the horizon, and all above it spread the glowing clouds of a fantastic sunset. Paul points at one sliver of color on a cloud formation and says: "That red is my favorite."

You can't help but wonder, looking down at your blue dress: "red is your favorite color?"

Had you been wearing red, this moment could have surely floated to the edge of romance. You can feel it, if you had been wearing red, Paul would have said "you look beautiful."

For the first time, your guardian angel has acted in a way that *seems* to be preventing you and Paul from becoming a couple...So which is it?

Then he interrupts: "What's on your mind?"

Getting yourself back on track, you *state*, you don't ask: "You really think I'll like it here..."

With a smile, "I'll see to it," he says.

You're still puzzling this text message curveball on your drive home. I assure you, you are absolutely right - it is better that you not become romantically attached. Get the job. Do the job.

Halmeoni

It's dark when you get home to your *Halmeoni*. She's watching a Korean singing competition show sitting on the floor. She waves for you to not make noise while coming inside. You take off your shoes.

You take your bag and your document binder to the kitchen table and look at the job application while she watches TV.

You search your memory of Paul's comments, looking for hints of flirtation. Paul commended the bravery it took for you to come to school in America. The last thing you remember is Paul saying that your spirit of adventure is like that of an explorer's.

You stare at your phone. What are these messages?

When your grandmother's TV show's segment finally ends, she mutes the volume, tells you to eat, and says: "your friend came looking for you."

Oliver! You forgot practice. You forgot all about Oliver. You feel terrible. You sit back down and send him a text message to apologize. You send a few messages because there is no reply.

Then you send the mystery person a text message, "Who are you? Where are you?"

You get a text response that reads: "the most interesting things in the universe are strange."

You're in the middle of writing "WTF" back to the cryptic babble when your phone pings another message: "watch TV with her."

Her?...Yes.

Your grandmother's TV show comes out of commercial and she gets excited, cute like a little girl. She waves for you that 'it's on.' You realize she's waving for you to join her. And watch TV with her.

How is this happening?!

You glance at the phone. You go and sit down on the floor beside your *Halmeoni*. She is very happy to have you there. She shares her fleece blanket from her knees to also cover your knees.

You enjoy how excited your grandmother is about these kpop wannabes singing cover versions of old Korean songs. She knows the originals and she sings along in some moments. Adorable. You're glad you came over to watch TV.

At the next commercial you ask your grandmother if she believes in guardian angels. She nods and touches her heart and says, "*had-abeoji*" - by which she means the grandpa you never knew, her deceased husband. She rubs your knees over the little fleece blanket.

Over by the table where your backpack and application wait, your phone is silent. No incoming messages from your guardian angel or from Oliver. You let it go. You and grandmother are spending some time together and you have no regrets. No regrets, you repeat to yourself in your head.

But everyone has regrets.

Don't Question Miracles

You wake up with regrets and they compel you to the coffee shop hours before your shift to apologize to Oliver. He is very hurt. You try to insist that you don't want him to cancel the show. You insist that you want to play with him.

He insists that you don't know how important this is to him. What he really means is how important *you* are to him. All you keep saying is that you'll make it up to him.

When Jess arrives for her shift with you, that's when Ollie can leave and he does in a huff. Jess asks "what's wrong with him," but she knows. You say you'll fix it, you two'll be fine, but you need to talk to Jess about what's been happening. You need to talk to Jess about your guardian angel - but she's getting ready for the shift. Putting on her apron, swiping in to the register, while you keep trying to get her attention.

Finally she listens when you say that someone is helping you hook up with Corduroy Paul, but all you mean is "connect with" him. Jess thinks you mean "sex." That stopped her cold, now she's paying attention.

You explain to Jess that you've been getting helpful text messages from a mysterious guardian angel. You show her the text messages. Jess' first thought is a joke: "Dum-dum, don't question miracles!"

You offer a guess: It's someone who's really close, because some of these things are very personal. "It talked about my grandmother," you say. "Like it knows. Whoever wrote these…knows all about her, and me."

Jess asks if it's Ollie. "No," you explain, if it was Ollie he would have reminded you about band practice. "It's somebody else."

What you don't tell Jess is that you're beginning to suspect that the texts are telling you about your immediate future. Someone can see your future. Jess has fixated on the hookup and asks all about what happened.

"Nothing. But he wants to talk to me about a job tonight. ...Like...how to answer these application questions in the best way," you stammer.

You know that sounds like a date.

"A date?" Jess yelps. "Tonight?! You dog!" But then it hits her, that you are likely, finally, moving on from the coffee shop. Her first thought is for Ollie's feelings: "you're gonna have to talk to Ollie." She reminds you to be gentle. You don't follow, oblivious.

Jess knows, even if you don't, that Oliver is in love with you. She worries that your obliviousness will end up breaking his heart.

All day long you watch your phone, glancing at it between customers, looking to see if you're getting any new messages from your guardian angel. The day drags by, finally as it gets close to your shift ending, when Paul's electric SUV pulls into the parking lot. That's when you get a text message: "Italian," it says simply.

You quickly show the message to Jess. She is excited and says "here come the fireworks."

You say, no, "what's next is private." You head outside and tell Jess to close up for you.

Jess waves, all coy-like, "be goo-od," she sings.

When you get into Paul's car he asks what kind of food is your favorite.

"Italian," you say with just a moment's hesitation...

"My favorite! Paul exclaims. So now you're confused again. Your guardian angel wants you two to get close, but not too close? Is that it? Who is in control of this relationship?!

You push these questions from your mind and ask him about "work" and successfully get him talking. All men are alike. They love talking about themselves.

Strange Italian

The restaurant is Italian for Americans, which is to say: mediocre…but that's to be expected in the middle of Texas. Your small talk with Paul is surprisingly comfortable, though your phone is in your lap on vibrate, you're ready for any tips. You don't need it.

Paul asks you what you think the most interesting thing in the universe is and you remember the old text message so you say, "the most interesting things in the universe are strange."

He squeaks. He can't believe you said that!

It soon becomes clear that "Strange" means something else to him, than it does to you because he launches into this speech about a team of particle theorists he works with which is doing particle-physics experiments about something called "antistrange quarks." He explains that the cutting edge of physics right now is exploring the component parts of quarks. You nod along and let him talk.

Like anybody else who is asked to describe their obsession, Paul fills up the evening with poetry. It makes him overjoyed to talk about the work happening at the *Desertron.* He beams, as you smile. Then later, when the food comes, he tells you all about Italy and Switzerland, how his team travels to the Swiss Alps to go to a particle accelerator there called CERN, and that you could go someday.

At one point you do check your phone and you realize you haven't received one text message. Paul notices, asks if everything's alright, he says he remembers you said you had an event -- Paul remembered, you didn't. Ollie's show! Paul asks for the check, and before you know it, you're back in his car and he is driving you to the Mithra Bookstore.

It doesn't look too busy inside, so you take a beat to thank him. He turns to thank you...You haven't reached for the door handle yet and you feel like he's going to ask to kiss you. Then your phone buzzes. He leans away again.

The text message reads: "Ollie." You cringe.

Paul wishes you a nice night and adds that he expects the finished application soon. You go. You wave and head inside.

The crowd is small because Ollie cancelled. There were a few other open mic performers, most of them poetry readers. Nothing drives a crowd away faster than a bad poet. Jess stares at you, disappointed in you as a friend.

Jess is not excited to hear any of your gossip. She tells you that you have got to talk to Ollie. Jess is angry for Ollie's sake. You feel so bad about Ollie that you offer to close up the shop, but Jess tells you to go home and call Ollie. But you don't call him - you wait to talk in person.

Oliver doesn't work again for the rest of the week, and in that time you prepare your application. Paul told you to send him your first draft of your letter of introduction. He said he would give you pointers.

Seven Years a Cobbler

But the wave of text messages you get are all you need. Each time you receive a text message with scientific help, the jargon sends you searching the internet to understand it, and you end up reading wikipedia for hours.

The text messages tell you to talk about being descended from brave explorers - immigrants. The messages say that the future is the single undiscovered space left anywhere, and that you, Betsy Kang, belong with those who will expand our borders into that space.

You take all these phrases verbatim and you notice that your guardian angel seems to be suggesting that there is an area of physics nearly unclaimed and unexplored which is a mashup of some disparate theoretical notions which you can barely keep straight.

Cyclotron particle accelerators, antimatter bosons, manipulated electromagnetic fields, you're not totally sure how these ideas fit together. But you smartly collect the texts into a bulleted list of interests that you introduce as being a new realm of physics that you wish to explore as one unified idea.

As you work on your application day after day, you keep going to class - but only the science classes. On Ollie's first day back at the coffee shop, he calls out sick. Talking with him will have to wait a few more days, but only because you don't bite the bullet and go over to his house. The next week, your essay draft is ready for Paul's review.

After you click send on your email, which you do just before dinner with *Halmeoni*, you get another text message. This one is in quotes, like a few of the previous texts which told you specific answers to Paul's flirtation queries. It reads: "I have more questions than answers."

This is a phrase you are supposed to repeat. But why? To whom? This text keeps you up at night for hours.

Paul is at the coffee shop the next morning waiting for you to arrive. He's excited. He peppers you with questions. He says he read your draft twice. He read deeper too, he read between the lines of your bulleted list and he assumes you have a specific theory which you are setting out to explore. He wants to know *how* you arrived at it. You let him talk.

"So you're suggesting mass-symmetry and the Higgs field, is to matter...what velocity-symmetry and a prism is to light wavelengths?!" You're not quite sure what that means, but you don't let on. He, meanwhile, is blown away. "How did you arrive at this?" You smile.

You respond that you have more questions than answers. But he pushes back, suggesting that you're being coy. He wonders what your mention of synthetic liquid molecules have to do with your wavelength-manipulation interests. Your innocent shrug doesn't stop him from rattling off a bunch of theories of where this new line of thinking could be applied.

Finally, late for work, Paul has to leave. But his parting words are: "seven years a cobbler." He says you are asking questions of the kind which Einstein asked while he was in school, questions which none of his professors could answer - this led to Einstein leaving physics and working in a government office job while no one alive could think through his questions with him. Einstein hated those years, stuck during the most fertile period of his thought-experiments. Paul promises you will not face 'seven years a cobbler,' as Einstein called it.

You wipe the counter and joke, "four years a barista." Watching his excitement, with nothing to offer but: "I have more questions than answers right now," does fill you with guilt. Paul is exasperated at your nonchalance. You hide that you're worried because you know you are cheating, and it is definitely working.

In The Door

That afternoon, you're in class when you get a phone call from a number slightly different than Paul's work number. A giant pit in your stomach forms instantly. You feel like they maybe caught you cheating somehow and you're in trouble.

The voicemail is from a colleague of Paul's who invites you in for an interview...today. It is very endearing that you waited through the rest of your class before racing to meet Paul's colleagues.

The next few text messages that come while you put on makeup start with basics: "pants, suit." But then they get a bit cryptically specific. Are they about feminism?

You're not sure. You write these phrases down in your new professional-looking leather legal pad notebook. You plan to read from them while you "take notes."

One hint from your guardian angel doesn't make sense to you at all. "Cinnamon," it says. You put that aside. Only a few of the other scientific hints require that you search the internet to understand the jargon more than you already do.

In these last few weeks, you have begun to focus more on physics. You have happily gone to your science classes excited to talk to the teacher after class.

You have started to see yourself as being very good at methodically scientific approaches to problem solving, and also you feel that you are good at grasping the processes of how high-level, nearly theoretical concepts, are turned into concrete mechanical action.

This is how the world works and you're deciphering the locks.

Yours IS the kind of mind that really should work in a physics laboratory. The excitement you feel driving onto the grounds of this facility is starting to feel right - deep in your bones. These text messages have been a miracle that has maybe saved you from "seventy years a cobbler."

At the *Desertron*, the woman who walks around the facility with you, again shows off the construction site where the cyclotron particle accelerator is being dug deep underground in a massive circle under three counties. The woman is named Dr. Gwen and she is older than Paul.

She asks you a few questions about what scientific principles you and Paul have talked about. She doesn't quite believe you when you say that your conversations have been more general than specific.

You mention that lots of your conversations have been about Italian Cinema, which is a mistake - too off-topic and the image probably gives Gwen pause. Gwen asks you if you know that Paul is married.

No. And you're taken aback…visibly. You get a little mad. And the anger serves you:

It dawns on you that Gwen might suspect Paul actually wrote the essay and is maneuvering you to be close to his office, because you are his toy! She doesn't overtly accuse you of having an affair with him, she is too nice, but there is something nearly judgmental about her head's slight side tilt.

Angry, you fight for yourself. You fight for you own your dignity. You don't even need to check your notepad for the text messages which perfectly establish boundaries and your autonomy, phrases which now are no longer cryptically specific about independence and patriarchy - now it is obvious what they are about.

You do not want, at all, to work with Paul. If you never saw his theory team again, it would not change a single thing about what you love - hard science. When you say this, you mean it. Both because you are intensely defensive against the accusation that you are a mere plaything for Paul, but also, why the hell not you?! Why shouldn't you become a genius? You should.

You state unequivocally that you want to work with a project leader who has a background in organic chemistry. This had been one of the notes. You add, a tad snidely: "is that Paul?"

Gwen shakes her head "no." And you say great. She smiles. Gwen says she can think of a few Projects whose leaders have an organic and inorganic chem background. She says she would be happy to escort you to meet these scientists.

You remember a text and smile, "I would love introductions, thank you."

She calls her Assistant back into her office and tells him to clear the next two hours. Her Assistant is at least five years older than you. And based on his shocked reaction, you gather that Gwen's offer is a VERY good and rare sign.

Cinnamon

You meet two project teams. One is led by a woman and one is led by a man. The woman's last name is Cinnamon! But Gwen brings you to the man first. You ask him for his thoughts on your cover letter. He reads the document that Gwen hands him.

He is intrigued but some of his questions are directed toward Gwen about the feasibility of using the *Desertron* versus a facility in Switzerland.

Gwen gives you a little wink when she quotes your previous fallback saying: "we have more questions than answers at the moment." You and Gwen thank him for his time.

The female team leader, Pam Cinnamon, is in a rush. She asks you to give her the gist of the idea. You do your best to quote it exactly. You even make the bulleted list sound conversational. Gwen watches you outline your cover letter with growing appreciation.

Meanwhile, Pam pinches her eyes closed with her fingers, her head flipped back as she listens. She smiles wider and wider as you talk. When you're done, she utterly geeks out on you. She is no longer concerned with her next meeting. This is very good.

Gwen doesn't need to verify your preference - you're beaming. Gwen surprises you when she tells Pam that you are transferring to A&M and that the *Desertron* wants to hire you as a project assistant, part-time. All of this is news to you! Pam offers that her team seems like a good fit.

Still nodding as you leave with Gwen, slowly chewing on the new thought that you're apparently transferring from your Community College to Texas A&M. All you say is, "I'm transferring?" to which Pam offers that the company will take care of everything.

Before you know it, you're sitting in your car in the hot sun. The AC blasts but your excited scream can be heard from across the parking lot. You stare at your phone and you think about writing something back to your guardian angel. You write nothing.

Then you receive a text: "Talk to *Halmeoni*."

The Rush

But instead you drive to the Coffee Shop. There is so much on your mind that your urge is to talk it through with Jess - talking with *Halmeoni* is not as easy, her English is not as fast as your mind when it's racing. Which it is right now.

You have not quite ever stopped thinking about these messages and who they could be from. Not a single text message you've received was false, or didn't come in handy later. The messages were sometimes helpful mere minutes after you got them! You're considering the theory that the messages might be coming from the future.

How have they known the future? Before you go inside the Coffee Shop you pause in the parking lot and you look around. You feel like someone is watching.

Inside, Jess is busy and haggard. Oliver avoids eye contact. He immediately takes a break. Jess tells you that you promised to play music with Ollie and she says, "we all make promises we can't keep... But we have to *at least try* to keep them."

You ask what you're supposed to do? She growls: "try!" and points down the back hallway where Ollie went.

You tell Jess that you have news about Paul and the job at the cyclotron, but she shuts you down with a hand. She doesn't want to hear it. She whips her finger down the hallway again. Go!

So you head out back to sit on the old picnic table. Ollie sits on the table top looking out at the dry creek. You immediately apologize. You ramble for a while about how your life is changing very fast and lots of big things got suddenly heaped onto you.

It looks like Ollie is about to blurt out snide retorts a few times but he bites his tongue. When you're done, finally, he says: "prove it." He stares at you. "These are words, it's air. What are you gonna do to prove it? What action?"

He gets up and simply walks back inside.

You rush home. You get the bass guitar from your bedroom and you're rushing back to the car when *Halmeoni* calls from the kitchen. You go over there, but you're itching to leave.

Your grandmother says, excitedly and happily: "are we talking *like this* today?" She means in the house, in-person. Curious...

But your mind is on your plan, you're rushing over to Ollie's with your bass ready, his roommate Lubu is waiting on the drums, you're going to surprise Ollie when he gets home! It's a good plan…

Halmeoni adds: "I like the phone too. It's good. So nice to talk."

You don't have time for this. "Okay...We'll talk when I get home. In person." But you've gotta run.

At Ollie's you help Lubu set up the drums and cymbals in the garage. They haven't been set up since the cancelled gig on Ollie's birthday. You have brought a bunch of soda and a grocery store cake.

While getting ready, you and Lubu talk. You're not all that close with him, partly because so often - like now, he is stoned.

You two talk about Ollie's birthday. Stoically he says we all get older. "Every day." College is going to be over someday. Your 20s are going to be over someday. And then your 30s, and your 60s and that's okay.

Then Lubu says: "You don't need to rush." You prod him to explain that he means one doesn't need to leave everything behind. You can take your time. You can keep playing music. You can keep Ollie. You should try. You may not marry him, but you are friends and you are only twenty years old. No need to rush.

And now that you know the truth about Paul and the wife he never mentions or the wedding ring he doesn't wear, you are definitely not going to be in a relationship with Paul. You're welcome.

When you take your bass guitar out of the case to plug it in, you notice that underneath the guitar, there is a little sticky note. You look at it.

It reads: "Time travel is possible."

The most recent message was "talk to *Halmeoni*." You remember and piece together that someone has been calling her on the phone and pretending to be you. The note in your hand says it all. It comes as no surprise that the writing looks like your handwriting.

With growing concern, Lubu watches your hand shake.

LETTER 2

FIVE YEARS LATER

Dearest One,

My thirtieth birthday was a dark grey drizzly morning. I woke up with horrible hair. I must have been tossing and turning again that night. I needed to get new pillows, I needed to change everything about that old bed in that old condo bedroom. But I changed nothing.

The shower didn't wake me up very much and I made *Halmeoni* breakfast half in a daze. Just some simple dakjuk porridge with kimchi. I focused on drinking my first few cups of coffee.

Halmeoni could tell I was depressed. She tried to make me laugh by breaking some pistachios using the bottom of her water glass as a hammer and sprinkling them into our breakfast. "Color," is what she said - she was adding color. I tried to fake a smile. I did appreciate that she was cute with me. It's not her fault I felt so stuck.

It was my fault. I never finished my Masters Degree. Paul pulled strings to get me a job as an Assistant Project Associate on his lab project while I was still taking classes at Texas A&M University. I had a lot of credits still to go and no direction about my thesis.

At the time, he and I were working late, very often at the lab, and he had arranged for the Employee Benefits Department to keep a one-bedroom suite on reserve at a nearby corporate housing condo leased for *Desertron* lab workers and guests.

It was during this time that he and I started sleeping together. Obviously he never talked about his wife. He never wore a ring. I never pushed him to take our relationship too seriously because he always got prickly. He'd say I was "crowding" him or demanding "emotional availability" he didn't have.

So I stopped having an emotional connection with him and we stopped sleeping together. I was overwhelmed by work, behind in my school, haggard from the responsibility of taking care of *Halmeoni*, and burdened by the pressure of hiding my secret life with Paul from our coworkers. I got depressed and stayed that way for years.

After a few years, Paul's project no longer interested me but I felt stuck. I had no bandwidth for exploring a different area of particle physics in my Master's Program, while at the same time working in Paul's old area of study at work. Paul's project demanded that I continually do mountains of reading and research in *his* area of expertise to keep up with him and his Lab Associates.

It was one of his Lab Associates who let slip that Paul was married. When she told me I froze. He had never invited me to his home. Every day for a week I wanted to confront him about it. I set my jaw and did not smile. For a week.

Finally, I crafted my question and asked him when we had a moment alone in his office; I lingered after a meeting and closed his door. "I know I seem upset to you. Is there something you never told me, something which could have caused me this pain? How does that make you feel?"

Paul offered a cavalier shrug, his eyes for a moment betrayed that he knew he'd been caught. But he toughened his face and said cooly: "If you're upset, it's because you had unreasonable expectations of our arrangement."

And that was all. No sorry. Not even one of those bullshit apologies, like 'I'm sorry <u>if *you're*</u> hurt.' He gave me nothing. Then, for every day of the next weeks, months, I felt nothing.

Until the morning of my 30th birthday, I ate *Halmeoni*'s fun pistachio chunks and softly touched the thin skin of her hand. I checked her doctor's schedule, I made sure the afternoon pills were set. I reminded her that the nurse will be by at lunch to administer her next regimen of pills and draw more blood for tests. With that, I left for another dreary day at the office.

The Loop

I arrived, as always, holding my work ID out the window at the security gate, barely stopping the car. On my walk to the entrance, I felt surrounded, increasingly, by a few new young women who were always showing up with new Masters Degrees and shiny PhDs.

I'd long since stopped caring about my hairstyle and my makeup at work. I was reminded of this when I saw all these girls with their shadowed eyes and fake lashes. My hair was easy, short, and on the morning of my 30th birthday, very unruly in back.

I got to Paul's offices on time and prepared my gear, along with the rest of the Associates, to head down to our small office room down on the beam level. After getting into our lab coats or protective layers - depending on which Lab Project we worked with - all of us Associates and Managers rode in the elevators down to "the loop."

Paul hired a new Administrative Assistant who remained behind upstairs. She was in college still and she was very pretty. Months ago I figured they were having sex. She calls me Elizabeth while calling everyone else by their title; Doctor this, or Doctor that. She downgraded my name with cruelty in her voice. Unfortunately for her, I no longer care.

One Shot

The whole *Desertron* facility was plagued by engineering problems. There were always work crews somewhere on the loop. The cement needed reinforcement, the wiring needed replacement, it got so bad at times that the circular tunnel itself needed to be re-leveled when there was buckling.

There is zero margin for error with lasers and beams, they need to strike sensor pads exactly right. In all the years here, nothing was ever exactly right.

The culprit was water. In Texas, oil fracking causes slight tremors and occasionally the sediment shifts. The *Desertron* was built to withstand these slight shifts, and to adjust to them. But these tremors also cause small fractures in the soil above the buried tunnel.

In Texas, seasonal creeks come and go with each heavy rain. Texas Creek water may sometimes run for a few miles in their dry beds before the water finds enough fissure cracks in the Earth to leave the surface and soak the earth underneath. This means that for the entire lifespan of this facility during the Texas rainy season, there were always leaks somewhere along the 54 mile-long oval tunnel. Some days, in some places, it rained underground.

Deep underground it was cold. We all kept sweaters and things stashed in our loop office closets. On my thirtieth birthday I wore black wool pajama pants that almost passed for normal attire, and two wool sweaters, one with a hood.

The dark grey drizzly morning where my condo was, grew darker over the course of the morning. But it was downpouring in the hills to the north-east. That rain filled the creeks which ran for miles. By the time it was raining at the office, the leaks were so bad there was chatter of cancelling all experiments for the day. Lasers and water do not go together well.

I was triple checking the wiring array into our team's mainframe when our snide meangirl Administrative Assistant patched a phone call into the sub-office line from *Halmeoni*. *Halmeoni* said she was confused, that she was seeing things, and that she needed help.

When I got off the phone I hurried to tell Paul that I had to leave. But he was trying to squeeze one more blast in before the bosses closed the Loop for the day. He asked that I stay for "one quick shot." Knowing this was never a quick process I said no. And I left.

With him complaining about me at my back, I went to get my things from our team's lockers.

I walked down a cement corridor that ran parallel to the loop. Every thirty feet, as I passed one of the open doorways to the bright loop, the loud buzz of the particle beam magnets bore down on my ears. The loud noise was the reason I wore earmuffs over my sweater hood - the wool of my sweater was warmer than the leather pads of those earmuffs.

Every thirty feet, the corridor had a few stair steps down, and then up again, dividing the walkway into stretches. In one of the stair-sunken sections of the corridor I noticed a trickle of water that crossed my path, the water was bleeding from under a metal doorway. Behind the metal doorway was one of the ladder shafts that had become a storage area. The water ran down a slight decline right into the giant sunken loop track.

There were plenty of water drains in the track area, but if a leak was particularly bad, I needed to tell Paul to cancel the shot. So my instinct was to quickly check. I should have just kept going, to go home to my grandmother. But instead I reached and turned the metal doorknob on the heavy-duty metal door.

All I did was turn the knob - but the massive wall of water pressing on the other side of the door blew open the door, the water knocked me onto my back and pushed me along the floor.

Five-hundred gallons of water tumbled me into the track. I found myself laying on the freezing magnet track that stretched in a nearly-imperceptible curve in both directions. I immediately knew I would lose my job. I knew Paul would blame me for the failure of this "shot" which I could hear warming up, even though I could tell that some of these magnet sections are shorted out from the sudden dousing of water.

Drowning in my depression, I was crushed with thoughts of my distraught grandmother, and feeling utterly alone and worthless - feeling as though I had wasted ten years of the prime of my life. I had wasted them. For nothing. Absolutely nothing.

The depression was immediately so overwhelming and so pure that it removed all other thoughts. The only thing in my head was this idea that…all was pointless.

So I, mad, and sad, and frustrated, and not giving a damn, stood up. I stood up directly into the beam. Did I know that I would probably die?

I think I did. But in that split second I didn't care. And in that split second, chose poorly. Cowardly. It was the worst thing I've ever done -or ever will do.

The beam of light accompanied an explosion in my ears. The flash of light was mind-blowingly loud for the duration of a half-heartbeat.

And then I awoke falling. In black. For three feet.

In darkness...my heart finished the heartbeat. I landed on gravel. I gasped for breath. Thank God, I thank God everyday that I kept on breathing.

Everything was black. But I was alive. The magnets were gone. I was on rocks and soil. My clothes were completely soaked with water. The dirt around me was dry. There was total darkness. I crawled over to the corridor where the flood of water had slammed me, but there was no tile. The walls of the tunnel were roughly cut into stone.

The particle accelerator was still under construction.

The Choice

After walking six miles in darkness, my hand guiding me along the tunnel wall, I only banged my head and shoulders into rock outcroppings a few times. Soon, a ladder shaft ahead appeared as a cone of light from above. I had to take off my sopping wet wool sweaters. Hypothermia would have come soon had I kept them on.

My shivering was bone-deep. It was difficult to find an area of the tunnel where I could get back to the surface unseen. Thankfully, it was still morning and the majority of the construction crew were not yet on the job.

Finally in the warm sun at the surface, I found a flannel shirt in the cab of an excavator machine. The work crews had their own trailer where they took their coffee breaks and punched timecards. Nobody saw me slip inside.

Inside the trailer, I looked through every locker and backpack for things that would fit. From locker #15, I stole a pair of giant jeans and I finally found a pair of shower sandals that one of the workers would find missing when he later tried to shower off the dust of his work.

I froze when I noticed a calendar on the wall. The date was 10 years ago.

The tunnel entry I escaped from was 6 miles along the track away from the main office where I worked - or would work. If I ran into anyone here, they would likely not know Paul. But nevertheless, I had to get out of there fast. I stole a few dollars out of a plastic "beer fund" jar. You will only need 5.

I hurried to the road but had to wait for a car long enough to get a sunburn. Finally a tow-truck pulled over for me and brought me back to town. I asked to be dropped at *Halmeoni's* house. I worried whether that was a bad idea, maybe I should go to the Coffee Corner. The driver said the choice was mine.

Choice. The word lingered. What we do has to be our choice.

My Gift

I found myself worrying that I needed you to connect with Paul and become a physicist so that you could go back in time ...because you are me. I worried that if you don't become a physicist - if you don't go back in time - would I disappear, like in movies?

But this was not some science fiction movie. This was real life and it was happening to me. Us.

I needed to think about this paradox. What I decided was that if I disappear because you get to have a different and better life than I did, I would be okay with that.

It occurred to me that if someone had given me good advice when I was your age, I wouldn't be here, in stolen clothes, penniless, riding in a rental car with a woman who kept looking at me with pity.

Do I actually know what's best for you? Should I push you away from the *Desertron* entirely?

But you are so good at science! I decided then and there that I would give you the choice.

But...I would never let you suffer. Pain was off the table - you will not fall into the same trapped life that I suffered, unhappily beholden to Paul. There and then I came up with a plan that would give you the choice.

I offered the stolen cash to the driver for the extra miles to where you are at work. The driver didn't want the money but she took me exactly to the side lot of the Coffee Corner.

Outside of the Coffee Corner, I watched from behind a car for when you went to the back to clean the bathroom. That's when I darted inside. I am sorry, I had to steal your tip jar. I needed that money to buy a burner phone. I was totally broke. Then I remembered Paul and the smug face he would make when talking about poverty being a choice.

Thinking again that it would help us both if you could connect with Paul and get work at the *Desertron* faster than last time, I hurried over to the DVD shelf and put "Atlas Shrugged III" into the DVD player. I thought that it might get him talking with you years earlier than it happened for me.

Betsy, you really should have known better. Paul was a libertarian. That should have been a red flag. Note to self: Never date sociopaths.

Also, I'm sorry that I stole your car keys from our basket. I had errands to do. I had to deal with Paul -- well, Paul's wife. The list of my worries was growing.

Trust me, you will not have to deal with any of this. That is my gift to you. Letting me borrow our car was your gift to me. Thanks.

A Plan

I ducked outside unseen. I took off the necklace Paul gave me. In my other hand were your car keys. My plan was to drive to Paul's house and give his wife the necklace and tell her about Paul's infidelity - my past, her future.

But I loved that necklace. I picked it out. I had kept it all this time not because I still cared for Paul, but because, simply, this necklace was mine. It was part of me. On a date with Paul I picked it out for two reasons: he was too careless to think of someone else and what *I* might like, and also because as soon as I saw it, I knew that it suited me perfectly.

At that moment, holding my necklace in my hand, I changed my plan. This necklace wasn't a remnant of my past, it was a key to my future. It was a key to your future. I did not go to Paul's house. Instead, I walked down the block to "Action Pawn."

Inside the dingy Pawn Shop, the hunched, bald dealer offered me $100 cash. I knew from Jess's brother that this man handled illegal sports betting. But I had no idea how any of this gambling stuff works. So I turned the stack of dollars around and pushed them back at the man saying that I wanted to place a bet against the Cowboys.

He looked closely at me. "You sure you wanna do this?" He warned me that the Cowboys are big favorites.

I came back at him with a bravado: "I want 500 to 1 odds."

He puzzled at me... "That's not how this works."

I stated plainly that "I bet the Jets win 52-3."

"I'll take that bet," he said.

Smirking to himself, he took the money and wrote in pen "Jets W 52-3. $100 - 500/1" on a small piece of paper. Before handing it over, he had to ask: "why are you doing this?"

I bluffed and asked him if he had heard of the "I Ching" - Chinese divination, numerology...He didn't know anything... and he also does not know that I'm not Chinese and have no idea either how Chinese fortune-telling works.

He shrugged acceptance of my excuse. I turned to leave, but before exiting, I told him I wanted to play every week. He snarked that he'd be happy to take my money.

I left him feeling good about himself. He would soon lose $50,000.

The Voice

When I got to the Coffee shop you were working the register, facing the door so I stayed outside.

I walked around to the back of the strip-mall where employees had their small patios and picnic tables for lunch breaks. I sat in the nice hammock that the Pool Supply company used and called *Halmeoni* because I knew for the next few hours nobody would be the wiser. *Halmeoni* let my unknown phone number go to the answering machine. I called out that it was me and asked her to pick up.

A moment later, she answered the phone. I could hear concern in her voice. You called her so rarely. Just hearing her voice gave me goosebumps. I began to cry.

We chatted for a glorious hour. I lied that the Coffee Shop was slow so I had time to chat and she was so happy about it. *Halmeoni* was making lunch, but I could hear her sit down at the kitchen table. I asked her about the lawn, and kicked myself...as if I hadn't just seen it that morning (according to her). She often complained about the ant colony in the dry patch, but I simply wanted to hear her voice.

I noticed when Ollie and you came outside the Mithras Bookshop and Coffee Corner, looking under the picnic table, searching for your missing car keys. You seemed in a rush, I made sure not to be seen.

I trusted you would get back to campus, no worries.

When *Halmeoni* was done talking about the ants in the kitchen, I said I would see her soon and that I loved her. It occurred to me, allowing people to talk about what they want to talk about is a sort of simple kindness. This gave me an idea.

My urge was to hurry you along. I did not want you to waste as much time in life as I had. If I could get you to prod Corduroy Paul into talking about himself, to get him reciting his standard monologues, you might be able to skip ahead, saving years of time, reach the fork in your road faster - the moment which I will build for you. The moment where you can choose your life.

So I texted you Paul's favorite book, the one he always loved to talk about, as being what inspired him to become a scientist: "The Panda's Thumb." I got no reply. I surely baffled you.

I had a moment to get a hold on my own bafflement. What had sent me back in time? Technically? Why? I needed to work on this problem. Because I would eventually need you to solve this problem.

So at 1:00 pm, when I knew you were in class, I was free to take your car with no risk that you'd notice it was gone.

I had 3 hours for my distant errands. You can imagine how tricky it was for me to tell Paul's wife that I knew her husband when I was in my twenties in the future.

That would surely not work. So, instead, I told her I had a work-related message for her to deliver to her husband. She looked dubious that I worked at the Particle Accelerator. I said I was with Executive Promotion and HR. She invited me inside.

When she returned with paper and a pen, I wrote a note that said, "Dr. Pam and Gwen are concerned about your A&M girls."

I folded the note and handed it to her. I thanked her for her time and headed back outside. I knew she would read the note. He would get what he deserved.

You Deserve It

You do NOT need to work for him to get your foot in the door. We'll blow him away and you'll immediately outgrow him. That is, of course, if you choose to perfect this time traveling experiment.

If you want to play in a band full-time with Ollie, I can help you do that too. I needed only to get you to the fork in the road where that choice is offered.

Then I drove over to the town library to get online and do some research at one of the free internet computers there.

I got a new email address and began writing notes before I forgot - what exactly were the conditions of that last "shot" in the particle accelerator. Maybe with a second, more controlled experiment, you might be able to control this result - how far back (or forward) one might travel. You might get credit for inventing time travel!

But I was getting far ahead of myself. The irony.

You were still stuck in school. By that time, I knew you were in class, in that dumb politics seminar, and I remembered the arrogant teacher. I sent you a shoddy, half-legible text about Rehnquist being a partisan jurist.

I searched the internet for the list of former political operatives who rose to the Supreme Court, but stopped myself. I didn't want you to get too interested in politics. It's best if you just drop that class.

Instead, I went back to my plan. I sent an email to Ollie's roommate hiring him to build a website for me -- I pretended to be from a scholarship foundation. I sent him the information and what I wanted the website to do and offered him $1000 to buy the website address and built the site.

He and I exchanged a bunch of emails where I wrote what the website should say. I knew he accepted crypto currency, so I promised him the bitcoin tomorrow if he would start work today.

When I got a text message back from you that simply said, "???" I didn't know if you were asking me to tell you more about the Republican judges so I had to make sure you stayed on track.

That's why I wrote "Panda's Thumb book."

"Who is this?" you asked.

I was not about to reveal that yet so I kept pushing you to read the book that Paul loved by "Stephen Jay Gould."

It occurred to me that you might need more help. I approached the large man at the end of the table in the library who kept looking over at me. I asked him, first, if he recognized me. When he said no, I was relieved. Then I said, "if I give you my number would you take a book out and let me borrow it? I forgot my ID."

He immediately agreed. Outside the library doors, the creeper handed me "The Panda's Thumb." I gave him the number on the bottom of the pawn shop slip. I told him that's where I work. I got his phone number and asked if I could see him tomorrow. He was baffled but happy to say yes to something that sounded like a date.

I had 15 minutes to get your car back to your employees-only spot. I hurried back to the Coffee Corner and hurried to put the library book on the bookshelf.

I gave your keys to a customer who was sitting near the bookshelf, lying that I found these random keys - asking her that she return them for me to the kids behind the counter because I had to run. She took them and soon gave them to Ollie.

I hurried away to go sit in one of the obstructed-view armchairs just on the bookstore side of the opening to the Coffee Corner, in one of the places that you Coffee Corner employees don't have to wait on or clean. What Ollie calls The Coffee-Book De-Militarized Zone.

You came in and found the book I left you. Ollie gave you back your keys. I could hear you and Ollie talking about band practice. I owed it to Ollie to be there for when people “happy birthday to you” - whatever happened the first time which I missed. I wanted to see it this time. I had to get a disguise.

After you left, not noticing the extra miles on the car, I went out back and fell asleep on the Pool Supply hammock. Thankfully it was a warm night.

Hide and Seek

The next morning, I was at "Action Pawn" before it opened. I called the big library guy and woke him. I asked him to come to my work. I hoped he hadn't called the number already. Usually guys wait a few days.

I waited for library guy to arrive before I brought him inside the front door with me. In view of the hunched bald man who owed me $50,000 I asked the library guy to wait outside, “I have to take care of a little business,” I said loudly.

The pawn shop owner scowled at me as the big man left. Then he gestured a small sort of - *ya got me* - shrug.

I approached. He said, “I Ching, huh?”

“Do you have it?”

He grunted. He told me “yes, but…”

He said that whatever system I used, he wanted to handle my bets against other gamblers for a 5% of my winnings. “The people you’ll win from, they may not be as nice as me.” I agreed, lying - again letting him think he would eventually come out ahead at my expense. I bought back the necklace and left the store. I never saw him again.

I had forgotten about the man from the library. He had served his purpose. To him I said, "sorry, I asked, he's not hiring." As if that had been my intention…helping him get a job. He grumbled, I left stifling a laugh.

By now, I knew you were at the Coffee Corner so I reminded you to read the book. I gave you the name of Paul's favorite essay: "piltdown."

With the cash I bought a computer. I put most of the money into a crypto account. I bought a phone and a wireless plan with cash. With the crypto coins, I paid for a rideshare to Dallas where I used cash to buy a fake passport - funnily, with our real name. In Dallas I bought clothes, and the contents of a day bag. I was dying to brush my teeth and take a shower.

I got back to town, rented a room at a motel and showered. Hiding behind my big sunglasses I went back to the Coffee Corner to the leather chairs out of your sight. Using crypto coins, I placed bets on the Cowboys' upcoming games on several sports-betting websites.

I opened an account on a website for angel investors. Because I didn't have $1 million in my crypto account yet, I wasn't able to make any investments in the small startup that I knew would soon become a phenomenon. I had missed out on investing in Google, I would not miss owning a piece of TalkingDraft.com. That's okay, by week 3 of the Cowboys season, I would be a millionaire. When Talking Draft goes public, a billionaire.

I thought about what we would do with this money. Then I saw Paul's electric SUV pull into the lot. I listened in on your conversation. Then, I heard Jess arrive. I heard

Paul invite you to see his office. He would probably try to get you on the roof.

I texted you, "don't wear red."

Once upon a time, I wore red to my first meeting with Paul at the Lab.

On the roof, when he said that the streak of red in the sunset was the most beautiful color, I joked back, "heyyyyy…" Coy, as if *my* red dress should be his favorite.

He did not roll with my humor. He leaned in and told me I was beautiful. I was floored. We nearly kissed.

Then our Italian dinner was not so innocent, and very soon we were sleeping together at the corporate housing that he arranged for me - any time I would need to "work late." Which was whenever he wanted to have sex with me. I should have stopped. I should have realized how wrong it was to have this relationship with my boss.

When I started working at the *Desertron*, I was stuck on Paul's team. I let myself get stuck. Before I knew it, all was lost. If you choose to go into the sciences, you will never be stuck. You will thrive with Dr. Gwen and Dr. Pam.

But that night, I felt dread. You were with Paul. He was probably flirting with you. I remember that feeling. I am sorry but I will break your heart. To help you. I could not sleep, so I took a car to *Halmeoni*'s house.

I just watched the flicker of the TV in the window, I watched from across the street, beside the bushes. I watched as you got home late. You texted me, asking me who I am. I wanted to tell you. Instead, I had to signal you I was somebody who knows Paul because I needed you to follow my advice about him. I needed you to believe me about Paul. So I wrote something that I know for a fact he probably worked into conversation with you: One of his favorite monologues about how "the most interesting things in the universe are strange."

So pompous, he really thinks he is an explorer. You are the explorer. He's nothing. I was still angry at him for the time he stole - from me, from *Halmeoni*, so I wrote a terse follow-up: "watch tv with her."

I walked to the motel, thinking about time and stories. I forgot to mention that I bought a half-bottle of wine. I thought about how writing is a time machine. It moves ideas into the future. Whoever invented writing gave us power over the future. This power comes with a responsibility to take heed from our past. The past teaches the future, but only thanks to words. Words are power.

Tech Time

These words I was sending you were dangerous, powerful.

"I am right," I decided. I was going to intervene. I would play you and Paul, and then I would teach the past - with words.

On Sunday, when *Halmeoni* and you go to Church, I would break into the house and intervene.

As I waited for the next Cowboys game, and planned my fork in your road, I pushed you further down the Paul path.

With some guardrails.

The next day, I could overhear from the Mithra Bookstore, the excitement in your voice as you told Jess about Paul - it sounded so familiar. I had a few uncanny feelings of regret and déjà-vu. But I was overjoyed to hear that you didn't kiss. So I ended up quite pleased.

I know he's going to ask you out - or he already did. It is worth the risk, I decide. I text you: "italian."

In the meantime, I've done some more research on my computer about the two things that are concerning me today. The first, is a memo included here which I will expand in the coming week:

1) What Happened To Me?

Knowns: There was something odd about the water. When I was laying on the gravel in the dark half-dug tunnel, dripping wet, the water that was soaked into my clothes smelled different. When I stood, some trickled into my mouth, it tasted like plastic. My soaked sweater was warm at first.

Known-unknowns: The flood of water that poured in from the doorway hit high-powered electrics and likely shorted some panels out - I must have landed on those broken ones because otherwise I would have been cooked. But the liquid shorting the power in those panels seemed to instantly create a vapor field from that liquid. The Higgs particles hitting those water vapor molecules formed a new augmented "aether field," as Dr. Cinnamon would have called it.

Unknowns: What was in the beam and what did it do? Dr. Cinnamon had been beginning to suspect that the Higgs field is a "universal aether" - that this field defines the terms of our existence. A wavelength field and a particle at once, the nature of symmetry locking everything into a single temporal state: Aiming forward.

Known - B: On that particular "shot" the beam path was loaded with Higgs and strange particles.

Unknown-unknowns: What were the frequencies of those strange particles? How did they change the wavelengths of the molecules in their path? That's something I want to find out. Did these manipulated Higgs-boson particles create a new field which short-circuited the connections that bind together the elements of the matter in its path? No. Because I was not rendered into a trillion atoms. Did it short-circuit the connections that bind together matter and its wavelength states? Maybe.

Is it possible that by adjusting an entire region of matter by creating an augmented Higgs field, what I did was adjust *where* that matter was in time? Was the synthetically adjusted water the fuel AND the medium?

Maybe. I did move the water back in time with me. It was massively humid in the cool dry construction tunnel - but only where I fell. The humidity dried out in seconds.

Known-Unknown: Why 10 years? Was it the precise amp charge, or was the precise length of time the augmented vapor field was bombarded. Was it the specific wavelength augmentation of that last shot that inadvertently specified where in time I would go? How can I test this in a scientific way?

What would have happened had I not been soaking wet in a thick steam bath? Surely death.

Did I decouple matter's temporal wavelength from the symmetry of its own mass? Whoa.

Was Einstein's outlandish idea right - that matter and electromagnetism are related to time? It would stand to reason that *what* was sent in time would not be solely a pile of atoms, but a collection of wavelengths. That's everything. Any matter in that Higgs-augmented vapor field would be affected, including my clothes and necklace.

I want to test if different kinds of liquids work in different ways. That was polluted rainwater. What would distilled water do? Ethyl alcohol? What was this synthetic liquid byproduct I tasted? I need to work this problem. I need to figure out why 10 years.

2) Boat

I need to figure out how to buy a yacht.

No Boat Yet

In truth, I planned to spend my money on you and *Halmeoni.* Sitting in the De-Militarized Zone armchair, my laptop plugged in, I worked online as fast as I could without a mouse. I transferred my money to Ollie's roommate Lubu and got a login to the backend of the scholarship application website where I would be able to review submissions. The scholarship's language was vague - the money was intended for young women in Texas. I considered narrowing it down toward you, literally someone exactly like you, but no need - I was in control. When I logged in to administer the website, having this control gave me an idea.

I knew your username and password for your cell phone plan. It wouldn't be current, but I would be able to see who you were receiving calls from. It might be able to tell me where you were. I did worry because it was getting late and Ollie and Lubu were growing anxious.

The open mic night crowd was a little larger than usual because of people who came for Ollie's birthday. I had to scurry far into the bookstore side to keep from being seen.

While other acts performed at open mic, including the usual bad poetry readers, I watched the excitement drain from his face every passing minute you were late. Jess surprised him with a little cake. I sang along quietly to "Happy Birthday to You." In the end, he and his friends left to go to a bar. For shame. I can't let you keep doing this to people who care about you. Betsy, be a better friend!

When I saw Paul's SUV pull up, I wanted you the hell out of that SUV. I texted: "Ollie." I wanted to rant at you, but I could tell from Jess' face that she would do it for me.

Food and Joy

The next morning was Sunday. I watched and waited for you and *Halmeoni* to go to Church. I know about the key under the loose brick on the side path. I slipped inside and smelled the house. Everything about *Halmeoni*'s house made me want to cry.

I had convinced her to sell and move in with me at my Condo closer to the office. She loved this house. She so badly missed this yard she complained about. I was so wrong about so much.

I looked in the fridge. All that food in all those tupperware containers! I sat on the floor right next to where she sits and watches TV. I saw the little sticky notes she left herself on the coffee table. I took one of the blank sticky notes and a pen and went to your bedroom. I put a note under your bass guitar that says "time travel is possible."

Then I got on to your computer and logged on to your bank's website and set up a direct deposit line between my crypto account and your bank. I clear cookies and shut everything down. When the money comes, you won't know who from.

In your school bag I found the folder where you put the *Desertron* application. With my phone I took photos of the questions. I put everything back. I left the key and went back to my motel room.

On the little motel desk, I started drafting an essay for you that would impress Paul, it would intrigue more than one Project Team leader, and it would get you an interview. And for good measure, I described you in a way that would also be a perfect scholarship application essay. The choice would be yours to make.

Over the next few days I began feeding you the essay. When I knew you were in class, I called *Halmeoni* and asked her to talk about places she might like to travel. Then I watched your email inbox - actually, your outbox, waiting for you to send the file to Paul. I had already done all I needed to do to ingratiate you with Paul. All that was over now.

Now, the job was to charm Gwen. A harder nut to crack - she had a stoic poker face. But there was one thing she did which I grew to love - a calling card - she always said the phrase: "I have more questions than answers." It was like a life mantra for her. If you say it to her, I'm certain she would love you for it. And that, it's fair to say, is indeed the right attitude to take into any new exploration.

I kept a close view on your phone records. When one of the *Desertron* extensions called you I knew you were in. They would never have called with bad news. I started peppering you with advice for the interview. I also worried that you might be given to Paul so I said things like "not theory, not team 12, independent - unattached - uninterested...stridently so. You have talent for hard science: organic chemistry, synthetics. ask for intros. Cinnamon."

I also kept nudging you to talk to *Halmeoni.* On the day of your interview I was as nervous as you must have been. I hoped that afterwards you would rush home to *Halmeoni* with good news.

I waited an hour before texting you to talk to *Halmeoni.* But I covered my bases by settling into the Mithra Bookstore blindspot with my laptop.

When you showed up after the interview, I watched Ollie leave. I could tell from Jess' face that she was in no mood to be your cheerleader.

I knew you would eventually either write to me or go talk to *Halmeoni.* When I saw you hurry back to your car and pull away, I had moments to spring the choice.

Ready Set Go

When I hurried into my motel room, I figured you were at home with *Halmeoni* and I wanted you to see the website I built for you…but before I could send you a message with the website's address I received a text message from you that contained the website's address.

"You make this?" is all you immediately wrote me afterward.

I had not planned for this.

What did that mean, I wondered.

Ollie's roommate Lubu must have recommended the scholarship to you.

What must you be thinking right now? You immediately thought I had set this website up?!

I didn't know what to do. I can only imagine how paralyzed you must've felt. Obviously you broke through the wall, you text me, demanding answers. Good for you.

I did not reply. I wanted to see what you'd choose.

It was torture to not write back.

Late that night you cut and pasted your introductory paragraphs about being a young explorer into the submission form on the scholarship website. The website alerted me the moment you clicked "submit."

I immediately selected you as the winner. The website sent you an email that I had pre-written - you were awarded a full scholarship to any University that admitted you as a student and you would be given a yearly stipend of $200,000.

Now you had to choose. You could follow your new direct path to refine time travel, or you could go a new direction entirely - with that money you could support yourself and *Halmeoni* to do anything.

Which would you choose?

PART 3

For The Last Time

In the cool subterranean darkness, Betsy Kang appears out of thin air kneeling inside a liquid bubble which pops and splashes down on her back, draining off her waterproof cloak. Rising from her knee as drips from her cloak's hood drop past her face, she mutters to no one: "All right. Last time. I mean it."

Twenty miles away, young Betsy Kang awakes in her small bed, muttering to her phone's silly song alarm clock: "All right. I'm up."

In the darkness of the tunnel, Betsy peels off her wet cloak. She pulls a flashlight, a dusty cellphone, and a wad of cash from one of the many travel pouches which wrap around her torso and she prepares to emerge, once again into the past.

When Betsy reaches the road a small car appears on the horizon and pulls over for her. A woman behind the wheel offers a ride. Only a few times does the driver ask if Betsy is alright, but the good Samaritan cannot help but worry aloud about why Betsy would be in the middle of nowhere.

When Betsy says she doesn't want to talk about it, the driver agrees, assuring Betsy that she's safe now. Betsy indulges the driver's savior complex with a few gracious thanks. The driver gives Betsy her card - her name is

Magdalena Moon. The business card is left on Ms. Moon's backseat floor when she drops Betsy off in Dallas.

Meanwhile in town, at home, *Halmeoni* and young Betsy's dakjuk porridge breakfast is as it always was: Perfect. Betsy's morning commute to the Coffee Corner is as annoying as every other day -- and all this is the same as every other loop. Later, mopping the bathroom floor of the Coffee Corner is just as tedious as always. She's the only one who ever does it. She begins to fixate on the swirling paisley shapes in a few large soap bubbles.

Moments later, outside the Coffee Corner, elder Betsy stands on the curb, her back to the shop's door, watching for Paul's electric SUV to approach. When Paul enters, parks, and emerges Betsy yells at him: "We're closed! Power's out." She watches him grumble his way back inside his car and back away. He leaves the parking lot. Victory.

Sitting on the closed toilet while the soap bubbles in the sink slowly drain, Betsy reads the label on the soap container, she wonders what causes bubbles to...be and stay bubbles. Little does she know - as yet - that a synthetic liquid bubble is her preferred method for time travel.

After the SUV takes off down the road, Betsy goes around to the back of the strip-mall. She slips silently inside the back of the Coffee Corner and approaches the (closed) bathroom door. Then, from one of her travel pouches, she pulls a folded envelope which she slides under the door. She quickly exits and hurries to the road where a rideshare car is 1 minute away.

Inside the bathroom, inside the envelope, young Betsy discovers a personal check wrapped in a letter. The check is from Lizbeth Kang to Betsy Kang. $1,000,000. The first line of the letter reads, "There is a cat purring on my lap as I write." Betsy thinks it's a joke. She asks Jess and Ollie if they're playing a joke on her - she doesn't get any more specific than that. Her friends swear there is no prank afoot. She has no idea what is going on.

Later that morning, young Betsy still has no idea, while standing behind the Coffee Corner counter – just waiting to get back to campus for class. But curiosity pushes her to search the internet for "Lizbeth Kang." She doesn't find anything too obvious and is left with no idea, still, what is happening. She has no idea the lengthy "To-Do" list that the elder Betsy "Lizbeth" was only just beginning to tackle for her big day.

Lizbeth's Plan

"Lizbeth" Betsy's first "To-Do" item began ten years ago. The night she won a "scholarship" with a yearly stipend, she began her plan. From Lubu, she found out where he got his fake ID.

That week, she got herself a fake driver's license under the name Lizbeth Kang - her photo was extra grainy and shaded and age-indeterminate. That ten-year old ID was in Lizbeth's leg-strapped pouch along with old cash when she appeared in the tunnel.

After emerging from the half-dug particle accelerator tunnel, her 10 year old phone already had several phone numbers pre-programmed - like a cash taxi service. She called for a car – Magdalena's – which brought her to

Dallas where she knew exactly where to go to sell the pouch of diamonds that were strapped to her leg.

"Lizbeth" opened a bank account with the old driver's license and deposited the $1.1 million which the diamonds had earned her.

Using the Coffee Corner's wifi, Lizbeth logged into the regular bank account that young student Betsy kept. Lizbeth watched the app on her phone, waited, but no deposit came through.

By 1:30, Betsy was probably in class, ignoring the "purring cat, change your life" letter. Lizbeth resisted the urge to text herself. The point of this cycle, she reminded herself, was to end the cycle. Lizbeth's impatience mounted. The last several years were spent running her own research laboratory, working through the problem: The "Knowns, the Known-unknowns, and the Unknown-unknowns" of time travel.

Ten years ago, the night Lizbeth had been gifted her scholarship, from herself, she wrote a text message back to the mystery number: "I choose both."

The instant response was a question mark. Then she proposed to meet and work together.

She asked her older self, Betsy Kang, to be her lab partner and fund an experiment – together they would perfect time travel. Young Betsy got a crash course in particle physics from old Betsy and they were amazingly and eventually able to control exactly how far backward in time an object would travel. The two built their own lab near the *Desertron* tunnel.

After many failed experiments, their development ultimately could control "when" an object would go to.

Additionally, they were also able to control *where* the platform would appear... with caveats: it could only appear along that exact latitude. (It took far too many tries to remember that the Earth was spinning).

After that, Lizbeth applied for time at the *Desertron* for her independent lab to run a particle shot. Target date: student Betsy's 20th birthday.

Waiting for Surprise

During the afternoon, Lizbeth constantly refreshes Betsy's bank app, waiting for Betsy to deposit the million-dollar check. Realizing it's not going to happen, Lizbeth calls Ollie on the phone.

Pretending to be a classmate of Betsy's, Lizbeth gently reminds Ollie that today happens to be Betsy's birthday. Lizbeth then adds Jess to a conference call. The plan hatched by Betsy's *anonymous* friend from class enjoins Ollie and Lubu, plus Jess, to surprise Betsy at her house.

The directive is this: they should gather her for a band jam. Not really band practice ("it shouldn't feel like work" as Lizbeth-as-anonymous classmate suggests). Offering to pay for the party, Lizbeth transfers a few hundred dollars-worth of Crypto to Lubu's account.

When Betsy opens her front door, the group yelling "surprise" in Betsy's front hallway includes *Halmeoni.* Betsy squeals and hugs everyone. *Halmeoni* offers everyone food. Betsy remembers that the *miyeok guk* is probably waiting. Betsy asks her grandmother if there's enough...

Soon, everyone is eating the birthday soup and, following *Halmeoni*'s lead - which came in traditional

Korean phrases - they each add their own blessings for the joy of knowing Betsy. The kind things she does. The great partner she is. Her sense of humor and patience.

Moved to tears, after another long and particularly strange day, Betsy repeats "gamsahabnida," and thank you, throughout the meal.

Then, with sudden intensity *Halmeoni* says "Cowboys." She scampers over to the TV and turns on the football game.

Betsy collects her bass guitar and everyone hurries outside to pile into Jess' car.

On the way to Ollie's place, Lubu lets slip that they got a bunch of food, they got wine, and they sold out of all the T-shirts - - that last one is curious. Betsy inquires and learns that Lubu talked with a woman who may have just forked over several hundred dollars.

Betsy nearly pulls the check out of her pocket but doesn't. It's probably not real...But she wonders…was the T-shirt customer Lizbeth? How could Betsy find her…

Home

Galveston Bay Tours offers helicopter tours and charters. It's not often that they receive a phone call hiring them to deliver passengers to an offshore yacht.

In the front passenger seat of the helicopter, *Halmeoni* holds her overstuffed luggage - a second bag of hers is also seat-belted into the backseat beside Betsy.

Betsy has only one small bag. In the bag, there are a few CDs that she and the boys recorded.

It had been very difficult for Betsy to track down "Lizbeth." Ultimately Betsy traced Lizbeth's deposits to an anonymous LLC company. The LLC was registered in Monaco through a shell company that owned a mooring in the Caribbean island of Bequia. From that clue, Betsy hired a courier to watch the harbor, and then to deliver her a message the instant the yacht or its tenders ever anchored there.

Betsy had to wait over a year. To now. But now she and *Halmeoni* see their destination in the shining distance.

The "Lunatessa" is a German-made luxury yacht, 164 feet long, with 6 cabins, a crew of 11, and an elevator to bypass the many stairways between decks – for *Halmeoni*. The retractable helipad spreads over the sundeck. From above, she gleams. Bold graceful lines join and stretch out to an incredibly long prow.

As the chopper rotors slow, the hired pilot helps *Halmeoni* out of the helicopter, Betsy follows with the bags - but she doesn't hold the bags long because a few crew members of the luxury yacht run over to take the bags away, offering insistently that Betsy allow herself to get taken care of.

The stoic crew escorts the bewildered and beaming guests to a glass-enclosed stateroom that looks out over the sundeck. The windows are polarized so that Betsy cannot see inside until she is close enough that the doors slide open automatically.

Inside gleams a beautiful, modern lounge with three walls of windows, a grand piano, and a bar where champagne bubbles dance in several waiting glasses.

Halmeoni enters first, and knowing what to expect does not overreact when she meets a woman who looks like her calling herself Betta, age 51, and then there's Bets, age 41, and Lizbeth, age 31.

The youngest Betsy, at 21, walks inside and immediately marvels at how well she will age. She feels relief and some pride.

"I brought enough CDs for all of us," she chirps.

"Welcome home," Lizbeth says, her glass raised.

"Geonbae!" *Halmeoni* drinks back the bubbles with glee.